Stan Lee's
SUPERHERO
CHRISTMAS

Dedicated to my daughter, Joan,
and to everyone everywhere touched by the magic of Christmas
—STAN LEE

For Abby, Ben, and Molly—my little superheroes
—TIM JESSELL

Stan Lee's Superhero Christmas
Text and illustrations copyright © 2004 by Byron Preiss Visual Publications, Inc., and Stan Lee
Book design by Arnie Sawyer Studios, Inc.
Manufactured in China by South China Printing Company Ltd.

For information address HarperCollins Children's Books,
a division of HarperCollins Publishers,
1350 Avenue of the Americas, New York, NY 10019

www.harperchildrens.com

Library of Congress Cataloging-in-Publication Data is available.
ISBN 0-06-056559-4 (tr.); ISBN 0-06-056560-8 (lib.)

2 3 4 5 6 7 8 9 10
❖
First Edition

Stan Lee's SUPERHERO CHRISTMAS

STAN LEE
Illustrated by TIM JESSELL

A Byron Preiss Book

Katherine Tegen Books

An Imprint of HarperCollinsPublishers

AT CHRISTMASTIME every kid's thoughts turn to the
North Pole. Can you guess why? It's simple. That's where Santa Claus
and his flying reindeer have their launching pad.

"It's time to deliver Christmas gifts to everyone," Santa said. "If I don't
get a speeding ticket, I'll be home by dawn."

BUT Santa had more
than a speeding ticket to worry
about. An old enemy suddenly
appeared. It was the evil Ice
King and his terrifying trolls!

"Attack, my little ones!" shouted
the Ice King. "The Protector isn't
here. That means Santa is at
my mercy! And the Ice King has
no mercy!"

"How will I bring presents
to all the children?" Santa asked.

"You won't!" The Ice King laughed.
"I've never liked children anyway."

"Then batteries will definitely not be
included," Santa's elf muttered.

YET all was not lost. In his hi-tech, state-of-the-art command center, the powerful Protector had monitored the Ice King's cowardly attack.

"Couldn't he have waited till I had my Christmas dinner?" the Protector asked. "But I have to go. Santa needs me. I hope my dear wife saves me some leftovers."

MINUTES later, Carolyn and Robert were just like children everywhere on Christmas Eve. . . .

"Shhh, Robert," Carolyn whispered. "We don't want Dad to know we're going to use his command center to spy on Santa."

"Not to worry, Carolyn," Robert whispered back. "He's gone. I saw him flying to the North Pole."

"You're right!" Carolyn answered. "There he is. But look!"

"Oh no!" Robert gasped. "The Ice King has Dad trapped!"

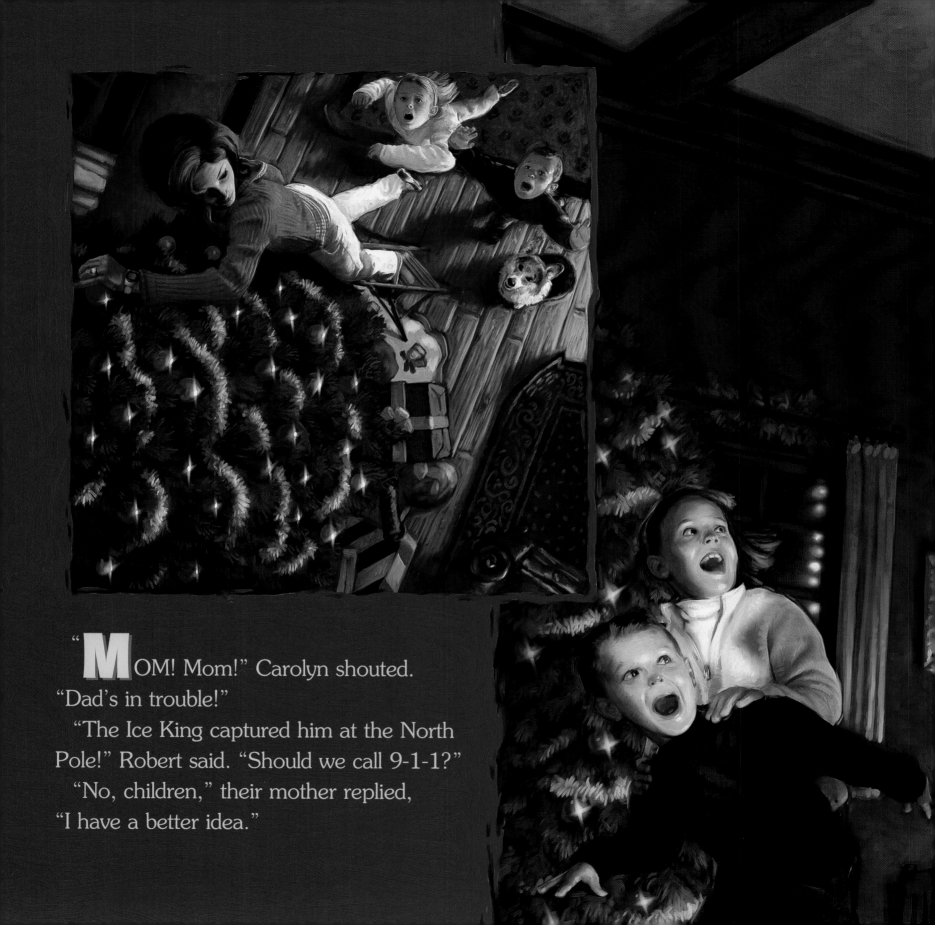

"**M**OM! Mom!" Carolyn shouted.
"Dad's in trouble!"

"The Ice King captured him at the North
Pole!" Robert said. "Should we call 9-1-1?"

"No, children," their mother replied,
"I have a better idea."

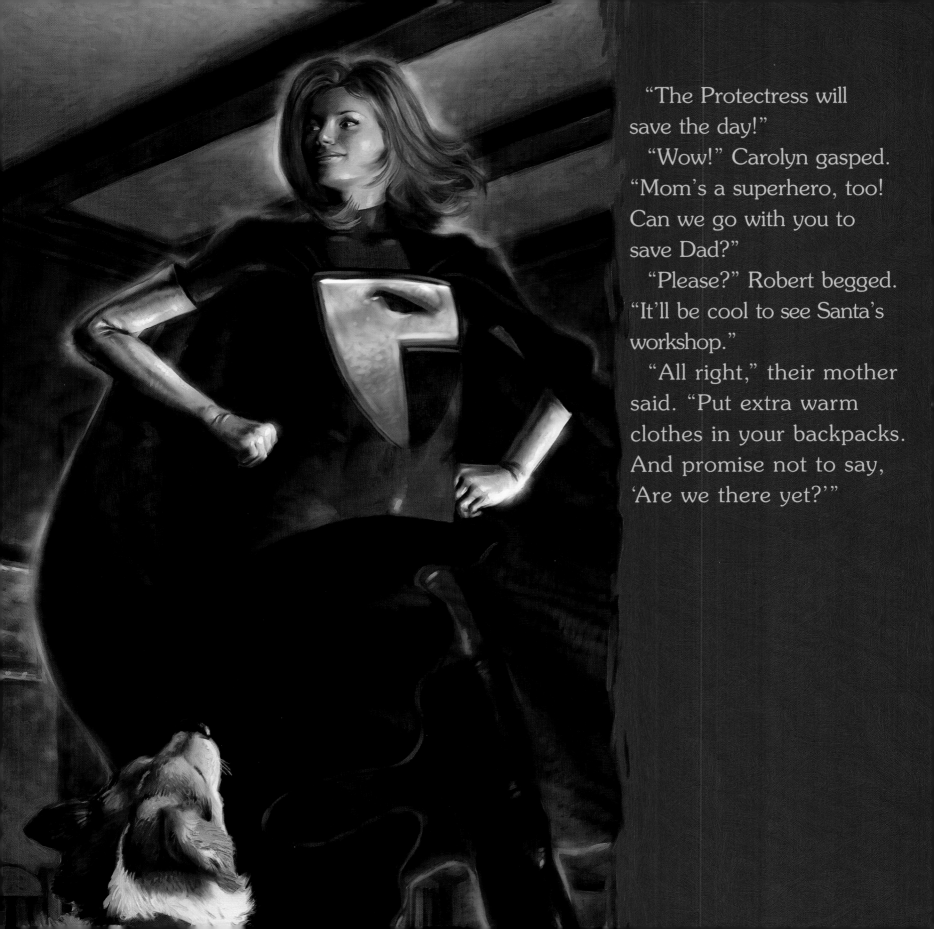

"The Protectress will save the day!"

"Wow!" Carolyn gasped. "Mom's a superhero, too! Can we go with you to save Dad?"

"Please?" Robert begged. "It'll be cool to see Santa's workshop."

"All right," their mother said. "Put extra warm clothes in your backpacks. And promise not to say, 'Are we there yet?'"

THEN, after flying at the
speed of imagination . . .

"We made it!" Robert cried.
"Mom's like a guided missile."

"But I'm worried," Carolyn said.
"She's attacking the Ice King
and his trolls all by herself. If only
we could help."

"You haven't a chance against us,
Protectress!" the Ice King shouted.

"That's when heroes fight best,"
the Protectress replied. "When the
battle seems hopeless!"

"**H**ERE'S one reason superheroes wear capes," the Protectress said. "Mine can catch the Ice King's frozen missiles—then hurl them back, making the trolls fall like bowling pins."

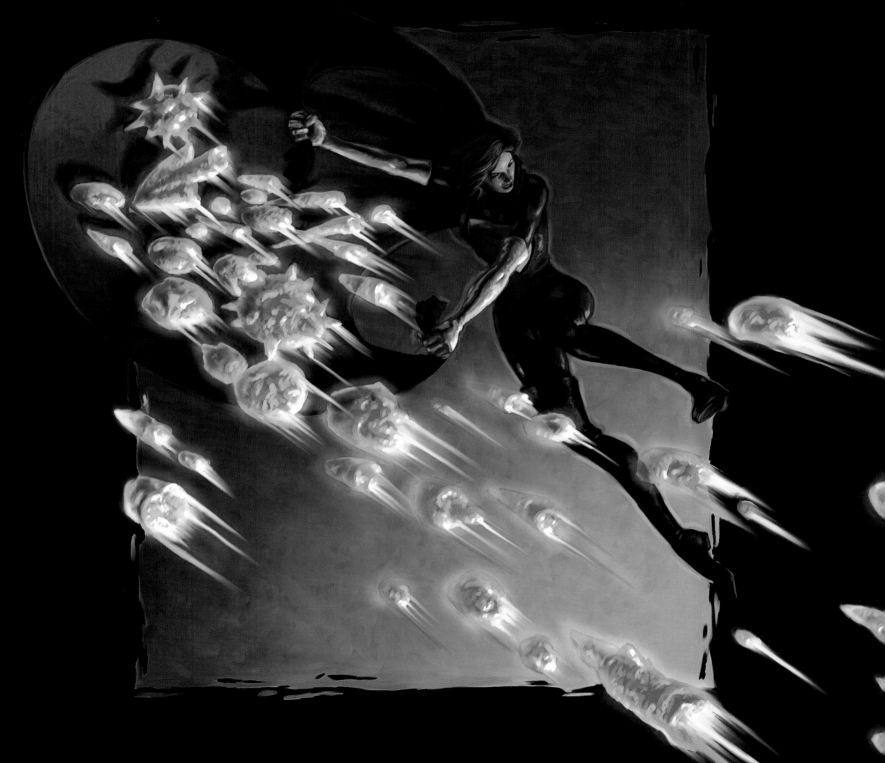

"NEXT, I'll shatter the Protector's ice cage," the Protectress said.

"No!" the Ice King shouted. "It's guaranteed to be unbreakable."

"Then tell the store you want your money back," the Protectress replied.

"You've freed me!" the Protector said. "There's still time to save Christmas."

"**I**'M not beaten yet!" the Ice King roared.
"Attack them, my ice trolls!"

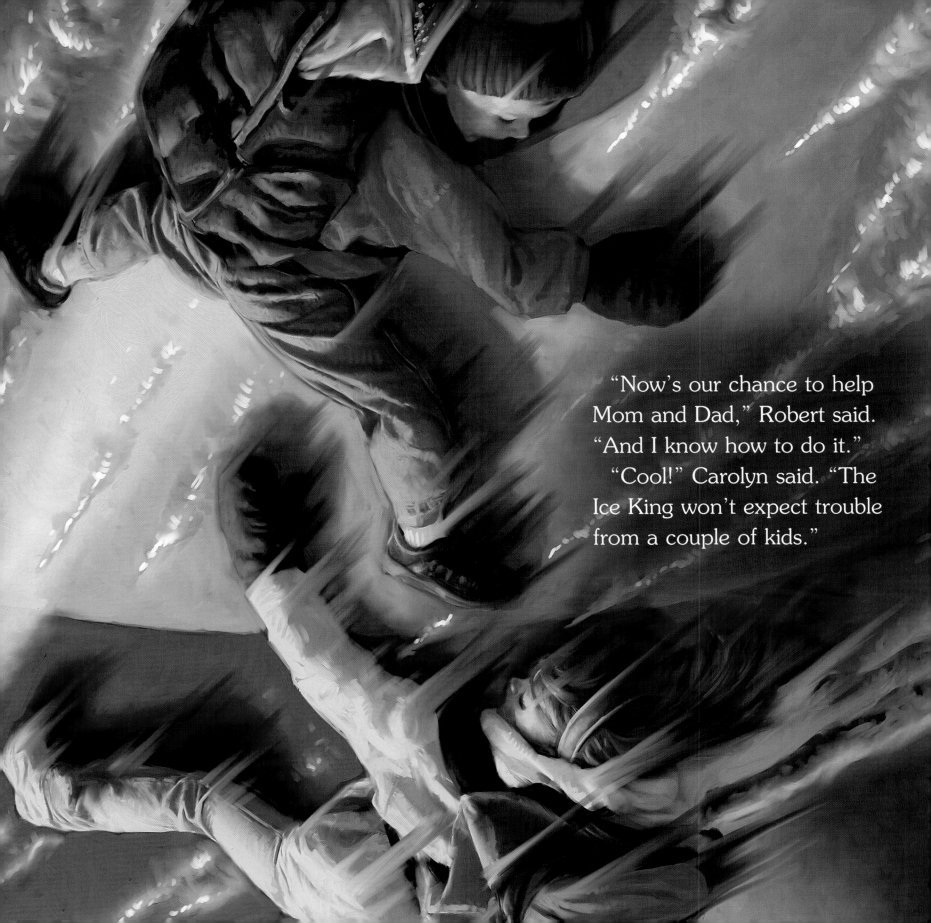

"Now's our chance to help Mom and Dad," Robert said. "And I know how to do it."

"Cool!" Carolyn said. "The Ice King won't expect trouble from a couple of kids."

"QUICK, let's empty out our backpacks," Robert cried.
"But they've got all our school supplies and everything," Carolyn said.
"Right!" Robert agreed. "They're just what we need!"

"We'll make a sweater pump out of my extra sweater," Robert said. "I never liked it anyway. All our staples and tape and paper clips and stuff will hold it together."

"Hey! Let's use this bag of rock salt that the elves use to melt the ice," Carolyn added. "It's just what we need to free Santa."

"LOOK!" the Protector shouted. "Santa's ice cage is melting—thanks to Robert and Carolyn. Guess we'll have to raise their allowance."

"The beautiful colors are like a sky full of rainbows," the Protectress added.

"Hurray! Now Christmas will be CHRISTMAS again," Santa's elf shouted.

"Let's get the reindeer and load my sled," Santa said. "There's still time to deliver all the children's presents . . . and I've got to think of something special for Carolyn and Robert!"

"We'll even get back in time to watch the cartoons on TV," Santa's elf added. "No wonder I feel like shouting."

"IT isn't fair," the Ice King said. "How come the bad guy never wins?
My trolls and I—we're melting away. It'll be ages before we can come
back to threaten Santa again."

"Hey, Ice King, did anyone ever tell you?" said an ice troll. "You

"Do you think the kids will like their Christmas presents from Santa?"
Carolyn and Robert's father asked.

"Not as much as our surprise," their mother replied.

"Wow!" Robert gasped. "We each got a superhero costume. I wish we had super powers also."

"I know!" Carolyn said. "Let's pretend we do."

"**H**EY, look at me!" Robert shouted. "I can control matter! I'm building a snow fort with its own slide just by waving my hands."

"Robert! I can control the elements!" Carolyn cried. "Watch me cover our tree with sparkling frost. We've become as super as Mom and Dad!"

"HAT a great present!" Robert said. "We're real superheroes!
"While Mom and Dad save the world for adults, we can do our thing,"
Carolyn said. "Look—on Dad's monitor! There's a town in danger!"
Together they shouted, "This is a job for— THE YOUNG PROTECTORS!"